Harry's
Great Escape

by Damian Harvey and Andy Rowland

FRANKLIN WATTS
LONDON•SYDNEY

Harry was fed up.

He looked at the children
having fun.

"I want to have fun, too,"
said Harry.

The children gave Harry

some food.

Harry looked at the door.

Harry got out.

He went onto the table.

"This is fun," he said.

But Harry fell into the sink.

"Help!" he said. "I can't swim."

"That was not fun," said Harry.

Harry looked at
the children painting.

"This looks like fun," he said.

The children went out to play.

Harry went to have a look.

He looked at the paints.

Harry went onto the paper.

"This is fun," he said.

The children came back.

He jumped down
and ran away.

Harry hid under the table.

"That was not fun," said Harry.

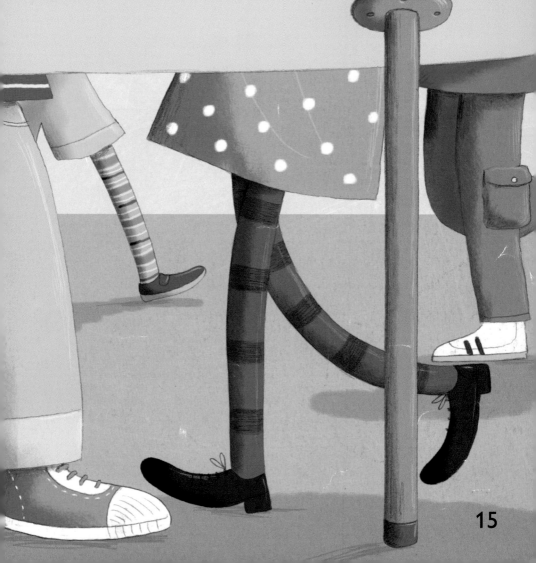

The children looked at Harry.

He was wet and cold.

"Oh no!" said Harry
and he closed his eyes.

Harry opened his eyes.

He was back his cage.

"This is fun," he said.

Story trail

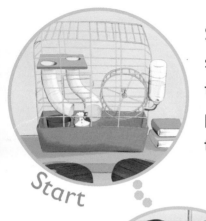

Start

Start at the beginning of the story trail. Ask your child to retell the story in their own words, pointing to each picture in turn to recall the sequence of events.

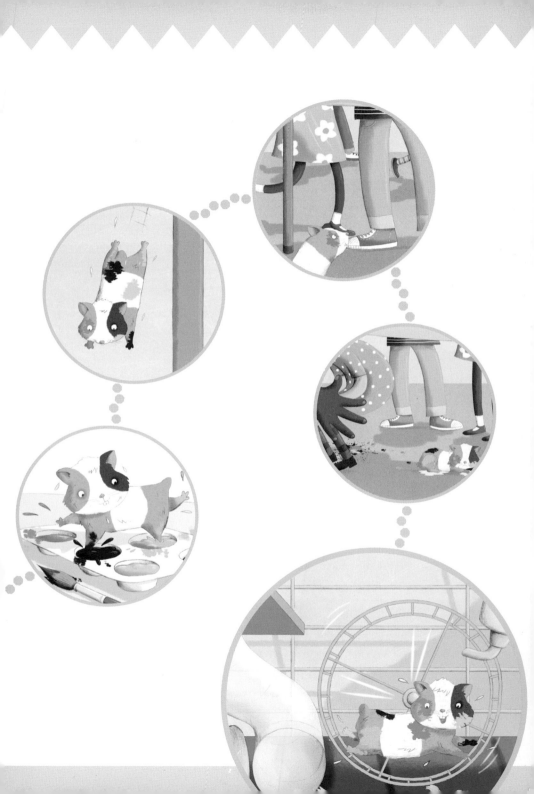

Independent Reading

This series is designed to provide an opportunity for your child to read on their own. These notes are written for you to help your child choose a book and to read it independently.

In school, your child's teacher will often be using reading books which have been banded to support the process of learning to read. Use the book band colour your child is reading in school to help you make a good choice. *Harry's Great Escape* is a good choice for children reading at Blue Band in their classroom to read independently.

The aim of independent reading is to read this book with ease, so that your child enjoys the story and relates it to their own experiences.

About the book

Harry is a school pet hamster. One day, some of the children forget to close his cage door. Harry spots his chance for adventure! But he soon realises it's much safer back in his cage.

Before reading

Help your child to learn how to make good choices by asking: "Why did you choose this book? Why do you think you will enjoy it?" Look at the cover together and ask: "What do you think the story will be about?" Support your child to think of what they already know about the story context. Read the title aloud and ask: "What sort of animal is Harry? What do you think Harry wants to do?" Remind your child that they can try to sound out the letters to make a word if they get stuck.

Decide together whether your child will read the story independently or read it aloud to you. When books are short, as at Blue Band, your child may wish to do both!

During reading

If reading aloud, support your child if they hesitate or ask fo
telling the word. Remind your child of what they know and w
can do independently.
If reading to themselves, remind your child that they can come a
for your help if stuck.

After reading

Support comprehension by asking your child to tell you about the
story. Use the story trail to encourage your child to retell the story in
the right sequence, in their own words.
Give your child a chance to respond to the story: "Did you have
a favourite part? What do you think Harry liked doing best when
he escaped? What didn't he like?"
Help your child think about the messages in the book that go beyond
the story and ask: "Why do you think Harry felt bored? Why does he
feel happy to be back in his cage at the end of the story?"

Extending learning

Help your child understand the story structure by using the same
sentence patterns and adding some new elements. "Let's make up
a new story. 'The class have a pet rabbit called Hoppity. He lived in
a hutch in the school garden. Hoppity was fed up. He looked at the
children having fun. "I want to have fun too," said Hoppity.' What will
happen in your story?"
In the classroom your child's teacher may be reinforcing punctuation.
On a few of the pages, check your child can recognise capital letters,
full stops, exclamation marks and question marks by asking them to
point these out.

Franklin Watts
First published in Great Britain in 2019
by The Watts Publishing Group

Series Editors: Jackie Hamley and Melanie Palmer
Series Advisors: Dr Sue Bodman and Glen Franklin
Series Designer: Peter Scoulding

A CIP catalogue record for this book is
available from the British Library.

ISBN 978 1 4451 6813 5 (hbk)
ISBN 978 1 4451 6815 9 (pbk)
ISBN 978 1 4451 6814 2 (library ebook)

Printed in China

Franklin Watts
An imprint of
Hachette Children's Group
Part of The Watts Publishing Group
Carmelite House
50 Victoria Embankment
London EC4Y 0DZ

An Hachette UK Company
www.hachette.co.uk

www.franklinwatts.co.uk

FSC
www.fsc.org
MIX
Paper from
responsible sources
FSC® C104740